Máquinas maravillosas/Mighty Machines

Motocicletas/Motorcycles

por/by Matt Doeden

Traducción/Translation: Dr. Martín Luis Guzmán Ferrer
Editor Consultor/Consulting Editor: Dra. Gail Saunders-Smith

Consultor/Consultant: Alex Edge, Associate Editor
MotorcycleDaily.com
Temecula, California

Capstone
press

Mankato, Minnesota

Pebble Plus is published by Capstone Press,
151 Good Counsel Drive, P.O. Box 669, Mankato, Minnesota 56002.
www.capstonepress.com

Library of Congress Cataloging-in-Publication Data
Doeden, Matt.
    [Motorcycles. Spanish & English]
    Motocicletas/by Matt Doeden = Motorcycles/by Matt Doeden.
    p. cm.—(Pebble plus—máquinas maravillosas = Pebble plus—mighty machines)
    Summary: "Simple text and photographs present motorcycles, their parts, and how riders use them;
in both English and Spanish"—Provided by publisher.
    Includes index.
    ISBN-13: 978-0-7368-7645-2 (hardcover)
    ISBN-10: 0-7368-7645-6 (hardcover)
    1. Motorcycles—Juvenile literature. I. Title. II. Title: Motorcycles.
TL440.15.D6418 2007
629.227'5—dc22   2006027790

Editorial Credits
Amber Bannerman, editor; Katy Kudela, bilingual editor; Eida del Risco, Spanish copy editor; Molly Nei,
    set designer; Patrick D. Dentinger, book designer; Jo Miller, photo researcher; Scott Thoms, photo editor

Photo Credits
Capstone Press/Karon Dubke, cover, 13
Corbis/Don Mason, 15; Michael S. Yamashita, 18–19; Nation Wong, 7; Ted Soqui, 20–21
Daniel E. Hodges, 8–9
Motorcycle Daily, 10–11
PhotoEdit Inc./Dennis MacDonald, 17
Ron Kimball Stock, 1, 5

**Capstone Press thanks Ervin Ohotto, of St. Peter, Minnesota, for his assistance with photo shoots
    for this book**.

Note to Parents and Teachers

The Máquinas maravillosas/Mighty Machines set supports national standards related to
science, technology, and society. This book describes and illustrates motorcycles in both
English and Spanish. The images support early readers in understanding the text. The
repetition of words and phrases helps early readers learn new words. This book also
introduces early readers to subject-specific vocabulary words, which are defined in the
Glossary section. Early readers may need assistance to read some words and to use the
Table of Contents, Glossary, Internet Sites, and Index sections of the book.

Table of Contents

Tabla de contenidos

What Are Motorcycles?

A motorcycle is

a two-wheeled vehicle.

It's like a bicycle

with an engine.

¿Qué son las motocicletas?

La motocicleta es un vehículo

de dos ruedas. Es como

una bicicleta con motor.

Parts of Motorcycles

A driver holds on to a
motorcycle's handlebars.
The driver uses handlebars
to steer the motorcycle.

Las partes de
la motocicleta

El conductor se agarra al
manubrio de la motocicleta.
El conductor usa el manubrio
para conducir la motocicleta.

The throttle and brake
are on the handlebars.
Throttles make bikes go faster.
Brakes slow them down.

El acelerador y los frenos están en
el manubrio. El acelerador hace que
la motocicleta vaya más rápido. Los
frenos hacen que vaya más despacio.

brake/frenos

throttle/acelerador

The engine rests
below the rider.
Big engines rumble
and roar.

El motor está debajo del
conductor. Los motores
grandes retumban y rugen.

engine/motor

Riders use kickstands.
Kickstands keep
parked motorcycles
from tipping over.

Los conductores usan
una patita para estacionar
la motocicleta. La patita impide
que la motocicleta se caiga.

kickstand/patita

What Motorcycles Do

People drive motorcycles everywhere.

They drive them to work,

to school, and just for fun.

Para qué sirven las motocicletas

La gente anda en las motos para

ir a cualquier parte. Pueden ir en

ellas al trabajo, a la escuela o

simplemente a divertirse.

Some police officers
ride motorcycles.
Motorcycles easily
get through traffic.

Algunos policías andan en
motocicletas. Las motocicletas
pueden avanzar fácilmente
en el tráfico.

Some motorcycles
are built for racing.
Motocross racers
sail over jumps.

Algunas motocicletas están hechas
para carreras. Los corredores de
motocicletas a campo traviesa
vuelan sobre los obstáculos.

Mighty Motorcycles

People ride motorcycles

almost anywhere.

Motorcycles are

mighty machines.

Maravillosas motocicletas

La gente puede ir en

motocicleta a casi cualquier

parte. Las motocicletas son

unas máquinas maravillosas.

Glossary

brake—a lever that helps slow down or stop a motorcycle

engine—a machine that makes the power needed to move something

handlebars—the part of a motorcycle that the rider holds on to and uses to steer

kickstand—a piece of metal that sticks out to balance a parked motorcycle

motocross—a sport in which riders race small motorcycles on dirt tracks

throttle—the grip or lever that controls how fast a motorcycle goes

traffic—vehicles that are moving on a road

Glosario

el acelerador—mango o palanca que regula
la velocidad de la motocicleta

campo traviesa—deporte en que el corredor de
motocicletas va por caminos de tierra

el freno—palanca que sirve para que la
motocicleta vaya más despacio o se detenga

el manubrio—parte de la motocicleta con la cual
el conductor se sostiene y que usa para conducirla

el motor—máquina que produce la energía para
mover algo

la patita—pedazo de metal que sobresale y
que sirve para apoyar a la motocicleta cuando
se estaciona

el tráfico—los vehículos que andan por las calles

Internet Sites

FactHound offers a safe, fun way to find Internet sites related to this book. All of the sites on FactHound have been researched by our staff.

Here's how:

1. Visit *www.facthound.com*

2. Choose your grade level.

3. Type in this book ID **0736876456** for age-appropriate sites. You may also browse subjects by clicking on letters, or by clicking on pictures and words.

4. Click on the **Fetch It** button.

FactHound will fetch the best sites for you!

Index

Sitios de Internet

FactHound proporciona una manera divertida y segura de encontrar sitios de Internet relacionados con este libro. Nuestro personal ha investigado todos los sitios de FactHound. Es posible que los sitios no estén en español.

Se hace así:

1. Visita *www.facthound.com*

2. Elige tu grado escolar.

3. Introduce este código especial **0736876456** para ver sitios apropiados según tu edad, o usa una palabra relacionada con este libro para hacer una búsqueda general.

4. Haz clic en el botón **Fetch It**.

¡FactHound buscará los mejores sitios para ti!

Índice